Margaret K. McElderry Books

An imprint of Simon & Schuster Children's Publishing Division

1230 Avenue of the Americas, New York, New York 10020

Text copyright © 2001 by Hilary McKay

Illustrations copyright © 2001 by Amanda Harvey

Book design by Kristin Smith

The text for this book is set in Didot.

The illustrations are rendered in pencil and watercolors.

Printed in Hong Kong

First published in London in 2001 by Hodder Children's Books, a division of Hodder Headline Limited

First U.S. Edition, 2002

2 4 6 8 10 9 7 5 3 1

Library of Congress Cataloging-in-Publication Data

McKay, Hilary.

Was that Christmas? / by Hilary McKay ; illustrated by Amanda Harvey.— 1st U.S. ed.

p. cm.

Summary: Now that both Bella and her cat are three years old, they are big enough to learn about all the wonderful things that happen at Christmas.

ISBN 0-689-84765-3

[1. Christmas—Fiction. 2. Cats—Fiction. 3. England—Fiction.] I. Harvey, Amanda, ill. II. Title.

PZ7.M4786574 Was 2002

[E]—dc21

2001030764

# Was that Christmas?

WRITTEN BY Hilary McKay

ILLUSTRATED BY Amanda Harvey

Margaret K. McElderry Books
New York   London   Toronto   Sydney   Singapore

Once upon a time there was a little girl called Bella and a kitten called Black Jack. Bella and Black Jack were too small to know about Christmas.

Then Bella and Black Jack were both one year old. They chewed up the wrapping paper and made lots of noise. They still did not know about Christmas.

Next they were two, big enough to run and climb. They climbed up the Christmas tree and it fell down flat. They still did not know about Christmas.

When they were three, Bella started preschool.
At preschool Bella found out all about Christmas.

Bella told Black Jack.

"Christmas is when it snows and Santa Claus comes on a sleigh pulled by reindeer. He has a huge brown sack full of presents for children!"

Black Jack hunched up his shoulders the way he did when he was cross.

"Will Santa Claus bring presents for Black Jack, too?" asked Bella.

"Of course," said Bella's mother.

At last it was really nearly Christmas.

At preschool they did a Christmas play with shepherds and angels and Little Baby Jesus in a bed of real hay. Bella was a shepherd and Black Jack was her lamb. Everyone clapped and clapped.

"What's next?" asked all the children.

"Santa Claus!" guessed Bella, and sure enough, the door opened and someone stepped in.

# SANTA CLAUS HAD COME TO PRESCHOOL!

Santa Claus looked just like Santa Claus should. He had a long white beard and a HUGE brown sack.

"Where are the reindeer?" asked Bella.

Santa Claus said he hadn't brought his reindeer because there wasn't any snow.

"No snow?" said Bella.

"No," said Santa Claus.

The children looked at each other, and Bella
(who was the bravest) asked, "What is in your sack?"

Santa Claus opened his sack and gave presents
to all the children.

But Santa Claus had not brought
a present for Black Jack.

Bella and Black Jack and Bella's mother walked home from preschool together.

"Wasn't that lovely!" said Bella's mother. "Wasn't that good! Santa Claus coming to preschool! Did you say thank you?"

"He didn't bring a present for Black Jack," said Bella.

"Oh, well!" said Bella's mother. "*Did* you say thank you?"

"And he didn't bring his reindeer and there isn't any snow!"

Then Bella started to cry. She roared. She roared and her tears got all mixed up with the rain.

"Whatever is the matter?"
shouted Bella's mother. She
had to shout because the noise
was so loud.

"Was that Christmas?" roared Bella. "Has Santa Claus been? Was that Christmas?"

Suddenly Bella's mother understood and she knelt down in the rainy street and hugged Bella and said, "THAT WASN'T CHRISTMAS! That was just the beginning of Christmas!

What we have to do now is . . . mail the cards to all our friends' mailboxes . . .

bake mince pies . . .

ice the cake . . .

hang up the streamers . . .

and fetch the tree!"

"And now is it Christmas?" asked Bella, when she and Black Jack were lying by the fire at the end of the day.

"No, no!" said Gran, who had come to visit. "Christmas is just getting started! Tomorrow we have got to . . .

go into town . . .
choose the Christmas crackers . . .

buy the presents for your
mother and father . . .

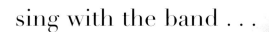
sing with the band . . .

shout Happy Christmas
to everyone we meet . . .

and ride home on the bus when
it's nearly dark and all the lights
are shining."

"Now it must be Christmas!" said Bella when she and Gran were home at last and the presents were hidden safely under her bed. "And *what* about Santa Claus?"

"What about Santa Claus?" asked Bella's father.

"He came to preschool and didn't bring Black Jack a present!" said Bella.

"Are you sure?" asked Bella's father. "Because it's not Christmas yet! You and I have still got to . . .

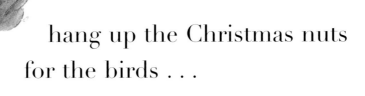

hang up the Christmas nuts
for the birds . . .

fix the tree lights . . .

eat sausage rolls hot
out of the oven . . .

mend the camp bed that Gran always
sleeps on and says she enjoys . . .

and make a snowman!"
"What with?" asked Bella.
"Look outside!" said her father.

It took all the next day to finish these things and Bella was so tired at the end of them that she and Black Jack had to lie down on the floor.

"Now," said Father, "we have to tell you about Santa Claus!"

"Santa Claus," said Gran, "comes when it snows . . ."

"It's snowing!" said Bella.

". . . on a sleigh pulled by reindeer. . . ."

"I knew he did!"

". . . He has a huge brown sack full of presents for cats . . ."

Bella hugged Black Jack.

". . . and children, of course!"

"But when?" asked Bella.

"Tonight!" said her mother.

"Is it Christmas then?" asked Bella.

## "Is it Christmas *at last?*"

"Oh no!" said her mother and father and Gran all together. "First you must leave Santa Claus a mince pie and a sausage roll . . .

a glass of juice . . .

a teabag for a cup of tea . . .

and a carrot chopped in slices for the reindeer.

Then you kiss us good night . . .
and climb the stairs . . .

and hang up your stocking . . .
and Black Jack's stocking . . .

and close your eyes
and go to sleep
until morning.

And then . . .

# THAT'S CHRISTMAS!"